Oh No—Not again!

Suddenly, Harry called out, "Oh no, Doug!"

"Wh-what is it?" I said, shivering.

"The Big Blue Bag!"

"Huh?" I replied. Blue bag? What was Harry talking about? "Where?"

"Over there. Mr. Beausoleil is carrying it. He just passed us on his way out."

I pulled my winter cap down over my ears and looked. "What's in it?"

"Ice melt!" Harry replied. "It means no outdoor recess again, like last week. I can't stand being cooped up any longer. I'm going cuckoo!"

OTHER BOOKS IN THE
HORRIBLE HARRY SERIES

HORRIBLE HARRY
Goes Cuckoo

BY **SUZY KLINE**
PICTURES BY **AMY WUMMER**

PUFFIN BOOKS
An Imprint of Penguin Group (USA) Inc.

PUFFIN BOOKS
Published by the Penguin Group
Penguin Young Readers Group, 345 Hudson Street, New York, New York 10014, U.S.A.
Penguin Group (Canada), 90 Eglinton Avenue East, Suite 700,
Toronto, Ontario, Canada M4P 2Y3 (a division of Pearson Penguin Canada Inc.)
Penguin Books Ltd, 80 Strand, London WC2R 0RL, England
Penguin Ireland, 25 St Stephen's Green, Dublin 2, Ireland
(a division of Penguin Books Ltd)
Penguin Group (Australia), 250 Camberwell Road, Camberwell, Victoria 3124, Australia
(a division of Pearson Australia Group Pty Ltd)
Penguin Books India Pvt Ltd, 11 Community Centre,
Panchsheel Park, New Delhi - 110 017, India
Penguin Group (NZ), 67 Apollo Drive, Rosedale, Auckland 0632, New Zealand
(a division of Pearson New Zealand Ltd)
Penguin Books (South Africa) (Pty) Ltd, 24 Sturdee Avenue,
Rosebank, Johannesburg 2196, South Africa

Registered Offices: Penguin Books Ltd, 80 Strand, London WC2R 0RL, England

First published in the United States of America by Viking,
a division of Penguin Young Readers Group, 2010
Published by Puffin Books, a division of Penguin Young Readers Group, 2011

1 3 5 7 9 10 8 6 4 2

Text copyright © Suzy Kline, 2010
Illustrations copyright © Viking Children's Books, 2010
Illustrations by Amy Wummer
All rights reserved

THE LIBRARY OF CONGRESS HAS CATALOGED THE VIKING EDITION AS FOLLOWS:
Kline, Suzy.
Horrible Harry goes cuckoo / by Suzy Kline ; illustrated by Amy Wummer.
p. cm.
Summary: While Harry's third-grade class is studying birds, the cold winter weather
keeps them cooped up inside during recess and Harry gets restless.
ISBN: 978-0-670-01180-3 (hc)
[1. Birds—Fiction. 2. Behavior—Fiction. 3. Schools—Fiction.]
I. Wummer, Amy, ill. II. Title.
PZ7.K6797Hnte 2010
[Fic]—dc22 2009030385

Puffin Books ISBN 978-0-14-241876-5

Set in New Century Schoolbook

Printed in the United States of America

*Dedicated with love to
my five precious grandchildren,
Jake, Mikenna, Gabby, Saylor, and Holden
who love to play outdoors!*

Special appreciation to . . .

The Appalachian Tails Pet Company in Glastonbury, Connecticut, for their help with my canary research.

Ms. Hall's third-grade class at Bedwell Elementary School in Bernardsville, New Jersey, for inspiring the director's chair.

Danielle Galligan, librarian at Hopewell School in Glastonbury, for her friendly reminders and help with my bird research, and for organizing two delightful lunches with the children. The conversation we had inspired many of the indoor-recess details for my story.

Kwan Kane, my Korean friend, who helped me with the dduk treat.

My editor, Catherine Frank, and her assistant, Leila Sales, for their enthusiasm, patience, and hard work.

My loving husband, Rufus, who inspires me with his sense of humor.

Contents

Harry the Canary

I know my friend Harry loves anything creepy, slimy, gross, or horrible.

He's been like that since kindergarten.

I didn't know that Harry would go cuckoo in third grade.

I blame it on the cold February weather, because that's when it started. Harry and I were standing at the end of Room 3B's line, *freezing,* waiting our turn to enter the Southeast School door.

Suddenly, Harry called out, "Oh no, Doug!"

"Wh-what is it?" I said, shivering.

"The Big Blue Bag!"

"Huh?" I replied. Blue bag? What was Harry talking about? "Where?"

"Over there. Mr. Beausoleil is car-

rying it. He just passed us on his way out."

I pulled my winter cap down over my ears and looked. "What's in it?"

"Ice melt!" Harry replied. "It means no outdoor recess again, like last week. I can't stand being cooped up any longer. I'm going cuckoo!"

When Harry first said *cuckoo*, I just shrugged it off. After all, the cuckoo is a bird, and our class was studying birds. They were on everyone's mind.

I watched Mr. Beausoleil sprinkle some ice melt over the frozen playground.

"Actually, the stuff looks kind of cool," I said. "Like orange Rice Krispies."

"You mean *deadly* orange Rice Krispies!" Harry snarled.

"You boys are taking too long!" Mary interrupted. "I'm not holding the school door any longer. It's freeeeezing!"

Just as she let it go, a hand reached around from the inside and caught it.

It was Sidney.

"Hey, Harry!" he said. "Guess what bird I'm doing my report on?"

Harry didn't guess. He hadn't started his report yet.

"A yellow el tweeto like you!"

Harry gritted his teeth, then clenched his fist. "Call me 'el tweeto' one more time and I'll smash your snozzola, Sid the Squid."

Ida and Mary giggled as we joined our class line in the hallway. Song Lee tried not to.

Sid stuck his face right in front of

Harry's. "Okay, I'll just call you . . .
Harry the Canary."

That did it!

Harry pinched Sid's nose and twisted
it like a doorknob.

"Owww!" Sid squealed. He jumped
on Harry and knocked him over like a
bowling pin.

Mrs. Doshi, the hall monitor, saw the
boys rolling on the floor.

"Okay, you two, that's enough!" she said.

Harry and Sidney immediately got up. Sid inched behind Harry's back. He didn't want to see Mrs. Doshi's angry face.

"I'm reporting you both!"

Song Lee covered her mouth.

Mary half-smiled.

I shook my head. This was not good. Miss Mackle, our teacher, had spoken to Harry and Sidney just last week about their quarreling.

Harry threw his winter jacket like a Frisbee at the coat rack, then stomped into Room 3B.

Sid hung his jacket carefully on the hanger and zipped it up. He even folded his scarf and placed it neatly on the rack. I think Sid knew he'd gone too far with the name-calling. He didn't want any more trouble.

After our teacher had a word with Mrs. Doshi, she calmly walked over to Harry's desk. I sit behind him, so I heard everything.

"It's time you and Sidney resolved your differences," Miss Mackle said. "I think spending your lunch hour in the principal's office talking with Mr. Cardini might help."

Harry sank down into his chair. That was more deadly than any orange Rice Krispies!

The VIP Chair

As soon as everyone said the Pledge of Allegiance, the principal's voice came over the intercom. "Boys and girls, this is Mr. Cardini. There will be no outdoor recess today. It's too icy and slippery on the playground. We don't want you to hurt yourselves. Happy Monday!"

Lots of people groaned, but some, like Mary and Ida, clapped. They liked having their Cute Club indoors. Anyone could join it, but I never did. Mostly they just made their little plastic pets walk and talk in different voices. Song Lee and I exchanged a look. We wanted to play kickball.

Harry stared into space. He was dreading something else: being cooped up with Sidney at lunchtime.

"Boys and girls, I thought it might be fun to add something new to our classroom," Miss Mackle announced.

Everyone watched Miss Mackle step out into the hall. A moment later she carried in a director's chair. It looked

like the kind they use in Hollywood, because the seat was up so high. The back and seat had wide strips of canvas. It looked really comfortable. The teacher set it up in the library corner. "This chair is for our VIP."

"What's VIP mean?" Ida asked.

"It means Very Important Person," the teacher replied. "Every day, one of you will be the VIP for Room 3B. You'll sit in this chair during our class meetings. You'll be my assistant teacher and run all my errands."

Suddenly, Harry sat up straight. The word "run" was like a magic wand.

Mary raised her hand and waited politely to be called on.

"Yes, Mary?"

"Are you picking people with the best behavior for the first VIPs?"

"No," the teacher replied. "I'm going in alphabetical order, and we're starting today."

"With first names?" Harry asked hopefully.

Miss Mackle chuckled. "No, Harry. Last names."

Then she set a large poster on the chalk tray. It was our class list in alphabetical order.

We all looked and tried to figure out which day we might get to be the VIP and sit in the director's chair. Harry didn't bother. His last name, Spooger, came near the end of the alphabet.

Mary clapped and cheered as soon

as she saw her name, Mary Berg, was listed first. "What a good idea to go in alphabetical order!" she exclaimed. "That's the fairest way."

Harry just rolled his eyes, and sank farther down into his chair.

Cutie Pie

"Boys and girls," Miss Mackle said, "please come to the library corner for our morning meeting." Harry was the last one to join us on the moon rug. Mary made a beeline for the VIP chair. When she climbed on, her legs dangled a little, and the chair wobbled, but she managed to steady it. Everyone could see her pink long underwear under her flowered jeans.

"So," Miss Mackle said, "let's talk about birds. Did anyone spot one last weekend?"

"I did!" Ida said. "We have a cardinal that comes to our bird feeder."

"I saw one of those on my way to school," ZuZu added.

Mary looked down at us from her VIP chair. "Are all cardinals red?"

Ida shook her head. "Just the males are. Both female and male cardinals have red beaks, but only the males are all red. I love their chirp." Then she whistled the bird sound.

"What a beautiful bird chirp you made, Ida!" Miss Mackle exclaimed. "Thank you. Anyone else?"

"Well," Sid blurted out, "I didn't just see a bird. I had a sleepover with one!"

Lots of us laughed.

"It's true!" he continued. "At my grandpa's house. He has a canary in a cage. Cutie Pie is my favorite bird in the whole wide world."

"Does he sing?" Ida asked.

"He sings a lot. My granddad got a CD with canary music on it, and every time Cutie Pie hears it, he sings more!"

"What else does he do?" ZuZu inquired.

Sid chuckled. "He takes baths in his water dish each morning, and he doesn't have to use soap to get clean."

Miss Mackle laughed.

"Actually," Sid added, "Cutie Pie is kind of like me. He looks in the mirror a lot and needs a night-light when it gets dark."

"What fascinating observations!" the teacher replied. "Thank you, Sid, for sharing those details about your canary. That's what I hope you all are doing—collecting interesting facts for your bird reports. Maybe you'll even come up with a creative way to share them."

Sid waved both hands in the air. "I saved the best news for last. Granddad said he talked with Miss Mackle and that he got permission to bring Cutie Pie to school one day this week."

Everyone cheered.

Except Harry. The last thing he wanted was a canary coming to Room 3B!

"What day is Cutie Pie coming?" Dexter asked.

"It's a surprise," Miss Mackle answered. "Now, let's see, did anyone else make some bird observations over the weekend?"

"I think Song Lee would like to go next," Mary pointed out from her VIP chair.

Song Lee was holding a piece of paper in her hand. "We have blue jays, sparrows, and an owl in our yard," she said softly.

"Is that a picture of one of them?" the teacher asked.

Song Lee nodded. When she held

up her drawing, everyone oohed and aahed. She had spent a lot of time sketching each feather on the owl.

"You're really making keen observations, class," Miss Mackle said. "Great job! Now, Mary, would you please line up the class. It's time to go to the library."

Mary loved being the boss. She knew just what to do. "If you're wearing lots of . . . pink, you may line up first."

Song Lee and Sidney chatted as they hurried to the door. "I want to keep this pet book," Sid said. "There is a good chapter on canaries, so I'm renewing it."

"Good idea," Song Lee said.

Mary continued her task. "If . . . you saw a cardinal, you may line up next."

Ida and ZuZu rushed to the door.

"If . . . you have library books, you may line up."

All of us did except Harry.

"Harry Spooger, did you forget your book again?" Mary asked, scooting off her director's chair.

"Yeah," Harry moaned, then dragged his feet to the end of the line.

POOKS

Mary led us briskly down the hall like she was the company commander.

As we entered the library, everyone read the felt letters on the flannel board.

Look for the new books in our library.

When Harry got to it, he lingered. It looked like he was fiddling with one of the letters. Song Lee waited for him.

"I'm sorry you forgot your book, Harry," she said.

"Yeah," he replied, "me too."

"That happens sometimes," Song Lee said. "What bird are you studying?"

Harry shrugged. "I haven't decided yet."

As we all filed by the return cart, Mrs. Michaelsen noticed Harry didn't have his book. She reached for a piece of purple paper, wrote down a title, and then handed it to him. "Just a friendly reminder that your book is overdue," she said cheerfully. "When you return it, I have a new bird book you might want to check out. It's about vultures."

"How cool! Will you save it for me, Mrs. Michaelsen? I love vultures!"

"I sure will."

Harry groaned when the two of us sat down at a library table. "Man, this is going to be boring. I can't even check out a book today." As Harry was talking, he played around with the purple reminder, folding it this way and that way until it looked like a cootie catcher.

"What are you doing with that?" I asked.

Harry shrugged. "I don't know. It's something to do."

Suddenly, Sidney appeared. "Did you guys see that flannel board?"

"Yeah, why?" I answered.

"It says there are new pooks in the library," Sid explained.

"Pooks?" I replied. "Huh?"

Harry had a toothy smile on his face for the first time that morning.

"I'll show you!" Sid said. Harry and I followed him.

There was the flannel board with a new message.

Look for the new pooks in our library.

Harry! I thought. *He flipped the letter "b"!*

"I know about pooks," Harry said. "I caught one last week with my pook catcher."

Sid stared at Harry's purple paper.

"Wow! What do pooks look like?" he asked.

"Well," Harry said, "I don't want to

spoil the surprise when you find one. But I will let you use my pook catcher, Sid. You just get down on the ground and look under things. Pooks are always hiding. If you call their name very softly, one might come out. They prefer being called Pookie though."

Sidney took the purple pook catcher and held it with his fingers. He crawled over to the nearest library shelf and peeked underneath. "Here, Pookie, Pookie!" he called softly.

I shook my head and walked away.

Harry was not bored anymore. He'd gotten Sid to play his game.

"Boys and girls," Mrs. Michaelsen called out, "please come to the nonfiction section of the library."

Everyone gathered around, except

Harry and Sidney. They were too busy looking for pooks!

"These are the shelves that have all the bird books. I am proud to say we have quite a wonderful selection. And over here on the computers are bird Web sites. They are ready for you to use. You can click on various topics like habitat, diet, migration, and even the sounds birds make."

"Neat-o!" I said, sitting down at the computer next to the circulation desk. I wanted to hear birdsong.

When Sidney started snooping underneath the librarian's counter, Mrs. Michaelsen came over to him.

"Did you drop something?" she asked.

"No," Sid replied. "I'm looking for pooks."

"Did you say 'pooks'?" the librarian replied. "What in the world are
pooks?"

"I'm trying to find one right now,"
Sid said. Then he took Mrs. Michaelsen
back to the bulletin board. "See?" he

said. "Harry told me all about them."

The librarian looked at the sign.

Look for the new pooks in our library.

"Oh for Pete's sake!" she exclaimed. She quickly took the felt letter "p" and flipped it right-side up. "That's supposed to be a 'b'!"

Mrs. Michaelsen looked at Sidney. "There are no such things as pooks."

"Oh, I knew that all along." Sid chuckled. "I like playing with pook catchers. Since I already have my bird book, it's something fun to do."

Mrs. Michaelsen stared at the pook catcher. She recognized the purple reminder notice. "Harry Spooger," she groaned, "I need to have a word with you in the back room."

My eyes bulged. The librarian's back room is behind the circulation desk. I could see into it through the glass wall.

Mrs. Michaelsen was scolding Harry. Harry had his head down.

Then he looked up and said he was sorry. That's what his lips said, anyway.

On his way back to the library table, Harry stopped by to see me. He didn't have a toothy smile.

"I'm lucky Mrs. Michaelsen still likes me," he said. "I told her I wouldn't mess with her bulletin board ever again."

"Good. *Pooks* was kind of funny, though," I said.

"Yeah, it was," Harry agreed. "You

know, Doug, I can't wait to see that new book on vultures. Those dudes are the king of birds."

Mary suddenly butted in. "Did you say vultures are the king of birds?" she asked, gagging. "They are disgusting. Vultures eat dead animals that have flies and maggots crawling all over them. When I saw one on the Discovery Channel, I had to turn it off."

"You missed out," Harry said.

Mary abruptly turned her head and went over to share her hummingbird book with Ida. Song Lee was checking out a book on owls. Ida had one with a red cardinal on the cover.

"You're going to gross out the class with your report, Harry," I said with a giggle. I didn't want him to know I would be grossed out too.

"Good!" Harry exclaimed. "Sometimes the truth is gross. Vultures hardly ever get sick, and they eat really slimy things all the time. I want to find out why."

At least Harry didn't get into any more trouble in the library. I was glad the vultures got Harry's mind off Sidney. Sidney wasn't thinking about Harry, either. He was still playing with that pook catcher.

While we were walking back to the classroom, Harry and I asked the teacher if we could go to the bathroom. "Good timing, boys. You can take the stairs right now to the basement."

After we hurried downstairs, I made a beeline for the boys' room. As soon as I took care of my business and washed my hands, I looked around for Harry.

He wasn't there!

Where's Harry?

I stepped out into the hallway of the basement. It was empty except for two first-graders walking into the girls' bathroom.

When I smelled cookies baking, I turned and walked toward the school kitchen. Maybe Harry was there. I hurried past the empty cafeteria and peeked into the kitchen. Mrs. Funderburke was having coffee with our gym teacher, Mr. Deltoid. They were laughing about something and eating chocolate-chip cookies. I knew what kind because I could smell the chocolate. It sure made my mouth water.

Harry wasn't there, though.

I walked back down the hall and headed toward the other end, where the gym is. As I got closer, I could hear footsteps. I stepped inside the gym and took one quick peek.

It was *Harry*!

He was running laps with his arms outstretched. He looked like a bird!

"Harry!" I called out. "There's no teacher here. You'll get in trouble."

"I have to run, Doug. I'm going cuckoo! Just two more laps."

I looked around the hallway. The first-grade girls were going up the stairs back to their classroom.

No one else was there.

"If Mr. Deltoid catches you, you're in big, big trouble!" I warned.

"Just one more lap!" Harry called out.

I began to perspire as I watched Harry run near the walls of the gym. When he got to a corner, he took a huge leap into the air!

Suddenly, heavy footsteps were coming from the kitchen. It was Mr. Deltoid, singing his bone song.

*"With the toe bone connected to the
foot bone,
and the foot bone connected to the
ankle bone,
and the ankle bone connected to the
leg bone.
Oh mercy how they scare!"*

Oh no! I thought.

Mr. Deltoid walked up next to me. He had a coffee cup in his hand. "What's going on here?" he asked.

Harry had just made it to the door of the gym, huffing and puffing.

I didn't move or say a word.

Harry did, though. "I had to take a lap, Mr. Deltoid. I go nuts on days when we don't have gym class. Especially when we can't go outside."

Mr. Deltoid nodded. "I'm glad you told me the truth, Harry. But you should have known better. You *never* go into the gym without supervision. I have to be here when you run around. What if you got hurt?"

Harry put his hands in his pockets. "I'm sorry."

"This had better not happen again."

"It won't," Harry promised.

Harry and I turned and went up the stairs to class.

Just when we got to the door, Harry started jumping up and down. "Oh man, I have to go."

I shook my head as he ran back down the stairs. As soon as I stepped inside Room 3B, Miss Mackle came over. "What took you so long, Doug, and where is Harry?"

"I'm sorry, Miss Mackle. We were talking with Mr. Deltoid. When we got upstairs, Harry had to go again."

After I sat down in my seat, I looked back at the door. Miss Mackle was waiting for Harry. Her foot kept tapping on the floor.

That was not good.

Boogers and Birds

At eleven o'clock, Room 3B was busy reading bird books. Everyone but Harry, that is. He was sweeping the floor for Miss Mackle. Mr. Deltoid had stopped by to tell her about Harry's laps in the gym. She didn't appreciate Harry's doing that. After she had another private talk with Harry, she handed him the push broom.

As I walked past him to sharpen my

pencil, Harry showed me the contents of his dustpan.

All I could see was a smashed grape and wadded-up Kleenex with boogers in it.

"Eweyee," I whispered.

Harry didn't cringe once. He just put his hand right in the middle of the debris and picked out a pencil stub and half an eraser. "These babies are gems!" he said, holding them in the palm of his hand.

I smiled as Harry stuffed his treasures into his pocket. This was the Harry I missed. The one who could be horrible but still stay under the radar and not get in trouble.

When I got back to my seat, Dexter showed me a picture from his bird book. "Did you know the loon is the best swimmer of all the birds that can fly?" he said. "He can stay underwater the longest and dive the deepest. It says it right here in my book."

"No kidding?" I said.

"No kidding!" Dexter replied. "Have you ever heard a loon sing?"

I shook my head.

"I have," Dexter said. "We go camping every summer up in Maine. There's a nearby lake with lots of loons. Those handsome birds make music as sweet as Elvis."

"Wow," I said.

Mary held up her drawing of a hummingbird so Song Lee and I could see.

"That's beautiful," Song Lee said. "I like the red throat and green head."

"The ruby-throated hummingbirds look like that," Mary replied, showing

Song Lee the picture in her book. "It says that hummingbirds have an average wing beat rate of fifty to fifty-two times a second."

"Man!" I exclaimed. "No wonder hummingbirds can hover so well."

At 11:57, Mary, the VIP, stood tall in front of the class and made an announcement. "Time to get ready for lunch. Please put all your materials away." She waited just like the teacher does. "Okay, good. Now those people who have cold lunch may line up first."

Lots of kids lined up with their lunch boxes.

"Hot lunch?"

I went to the end of the line with Harry and Sidney.

It was almost time for their deadly

appointment with the principal.

Both of them would have to sit in his office and be good for one whole hour.

One whole hour?

That meant sixty full minutes, or three thousand six hundred seconds!

"Whoa," I sighed.

As we walked downstairs to the cafeteria, Sidney had his canary book tucked under his arm. I was glad he had left his purple pook catcher in his desk. Neither one of them said a word.

Harry looked like he was about to be sick.

Harry Goes to Prison

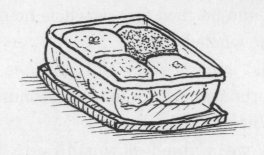

Mrs. Funderburke, the head cook, greeted us all with a big smile. "Got your favorite vegetable today, Harry. Broccoli!"

Harry didn't even look up. He just stared at the macaroni and cheese.

It was yellow, like a canary.

I reached for a dish of apple crisp and orange slices and put it on my tray. I tried to think of a few words I could say to Harry before he went off to prison. That's where it seemed like he was going, anyway.

As we got to the end of the serving line and picked up our milk cartons, I gave a three-finger salute to Harry. "Be brave," I said.

Harry didn't salute me back like usual. This was pure torture for him.

I watched Sid and Harry carry their trays out of the cafeteria, then sat down at Room 3B's table. "I feel bad for Harry," I sighed.

"Me too," Song Lee said. She sat across the table from me. She always brought Korean food, like kimchi, a cabbage dish, for lunch. Today she had an extra square plastic container.

"I don't feel sorry for Harry!" Mary

snapped. "He broke a school rule." She opened up a plastic box in her lunch bag and took out a whole-wheat sandwich. I knew what it was by its smell. Egg and pickles.

"What's that?" Mary asked when Song Lee took off the lid to her second container.

"Dduk," Song Lee said. "Rice-and-bean cakes."

"They look like little dumplings," Mary replied.

"They are very sweet." Song Lee pointed to the first row of light ones. "These two are rolled in sesame seed. The other two are rolled in cinnamon sugar. We made them for my cousin's wedding."

I ate half my mac and cheese before I joined their conversation.

"Do you think we should try to visit Harry?" I asked.

Song Lee immediately nodded yes. "Harry *and* Sidney need a friend."

"They do," I agreed. "And maybe if they saw us, their moods might improve, and they wouldn't do anything . . . "

" . . . stupid?" Mary answered.

"Yeah," I groaned.

"You have to get permission from Mrs. Doshi to go to the office," Mary snapped.

"I know," I said. "I was thinking . . . If I brought something to the school secretary, like a birthday cupcake, that would be a good excuse. Lots of kids do that."

"True," Mary said. "But it's not your birthday. And we don't have a cupcake."

"Maybe," Song Lee suggested, "we could offer Mrs. Carpenter and Mr. Cardini some sweet dduk."

"What a good idea!" I said.

"You're giving all of those rice cakes away?" Mary gasped. I think she wanted to try one.

"They might help us help Harry," Song Lee answered, "and Sidney."

"She's right," I agreed.

Song Lee bravely raised her hand.

Mrs. Doshi appeared right away. "How are you doing, Song Lee?" she asked.

"Fine, thank you. I would like to offer you some dduk."

Mrs. Doshi looked at the two rows of rice cakes. "How lovely!"

She took a light one and bit into it.

"Mmmmm, sesame seed. What is that filling in the center?"

"Bean curd and brown sugar," Song Lee said, beaming. Then she popped the big question. "May I bring one to the principal and school secretary?"

"Oh, they would love that!" Mrs. Doshi replied. "That would make their day!"

"Can Doug go with me?" Song Lee asked softly.

Mrs. Doshi smiled. "Sure. Hurry back."

As soon as the aide left, I jumped out of my seat. "You did it!" I exclaimed.

Song Lee put the lid back on her plastic container and smiled. Then we hurried out of the cafeteria together. As we scooted up the stairs, I had three horrible thoughts.

What if Harry slugged
Sidney and knocked down
the framed pictures
hanging on the wall?
What if Harry dumped
macaroni and cheese on top
of Sid's head?
What if Harry put
broccoli spears in his nos-
trils and barked like a walrus?
It seemed to take forever for
us to get to the first floor. Finally,
we turned left to go down the long
hallway. At the end, we could see the
sign that said:

OFFICE THIS WAY

We turned left again. The office was
just two doors down.

As we got closer, we could see through the glass window. There was the school secretary, typing on her computer. Her blonde hair was neatly packed on top of her head in a bun. She had lots of little stuffed animals lined up on her shelf. She collected them. We went right up to her desk.

"Hello, Mrs. Carpenter," we said.

"Hello, Song Lee and Doug," she answered.

"I want to offer you and Mr. Cardini some sweet dduk," Song Lee said with a big smile. Then she added, "They are rice-and-bean cakes from a Korean wedding."

"Oh, how exquisite!" Mrs. Carpenter said. She reached into her bottom drawer and pulled out two little paper plates. I noticed she had napkins and sugar packets too. Very carefully, she picked out a rice cake and put it on a plate on her desk. Then she did it again. "I'll bring this one in to Mr. Cardini right now."

We watched the secretary knock twice on the principal's door, then enter his office. We were disappointed that she closed the door behind her.

Song Lee and I crossed our fingers.

Suddenly, there was a very loud noise and screaming! Song Lee and I looked at each other.

Boom! Bam! Then someone shouted, "Oh no!"

What was going on in the principal's office?

Finally, after one long minute of weird sounds and a lot of footsteps, everything turned quiet.

The door opened and Mrs. Carpenter came out. Her neat yellow bun was all messed up. There were even a few tiny black-and-white blotchy things in her hair.

"Are you okay?" Song Lee asked.

Mrs. Carpenter plopped down in her chair and took a deep breath. "Fine, now."

"What happened?" I said.

"There was quite a commotion in the principal's office. I'm glad you missed the pandemonium."

Song Lee and I exchanged a worried look.

"Pan-de—what?" I repeated.

"Pandemonium. It means an uproar. But it's nothing for you two to worry about."

"Was . . . Harry involved in that pan-de-mon-i-um?" Song Lee politely asked.

"Yes," Mrs. Carpenter said. "He and Sidney. But that's top secret. Mr. Cardini is taking care of things. Thank you very much for the delicious rice cakes. I'm going to enjoy mine with a cup of tea. You two should go back to lunch now."

Song Lee and I exchanged a worried look as we hurried down the hall.

"Do you think Harry's going to be kicked out of school?" I asked.

"No," Song Lee replied. "Harry has a good heart."

I said a silent prayer for him. I hoped that Mr. Cardini would forgive Harry for all the problems he had caused today.

When we got to the cafeteria, Mary was eagerly waiting for us at Room 3B's table. "What happened? Did you see them?"

"No," I groaned. "We went to the

office. Song Lee gave up her dduk just to help Harry and Sidney, but we never got to see them."

"We do know the pandemonium stopped," Song Lee added.

Mary lowered her eyebrows. She seemed curious about the word until she saw the plastic container in Song Lee's hand. There was one rice cake left. "Aren't you going to eat that one?" she asked.

Song Lee shook her head. She wasn't hungry. "You can have it, Mary."

"Gee, thanks! Mmmm... cinnamon," she said, popping it into her mouth and licking her fingers.

Mary was the only one happy about the way things had turned out.

Harry and Sidney Return

When we got back to Room 3B for indoor recess, I didn't play Battleship with Dexter or build a LEGO empire with ZuZu or join the Cute Club.

I just sat at my desk, watching the wall clock tick. Harry and Sidney would be returning in about fifteen minutes.

Why did Harry have to get in so much trouble? Why couldn't he just go back to being plain horrible?

Song Lee was making an owl book-mark for Harry.

As I watched her draw, I drummed my fingers on the top of my desk.

Mary didn't help my nerves any. She was moving a little plastic dog along the edge of her desk, making it talk in a low voice. "Hmmmm . . . I wonder how Harry and Sidney are doing?"

Ida replied in a high voice, pretending to talk for the little plastic cat in her hand. "They should be getting back soon."

Suddenly, Mr. Cardini stepped into the room.

"Boys and girls, I want you to put everything away and return to your seats."

That was easy for me. I hadn't moved an inch or made a mess.

"I have an important announcement to make," the principal continued in a serious voice.

Miss Mackle quickly helped a few children put their board-game pieces away.

When everyone was sitting quietly, the principal motioned to someone just outside the door. Harry and Sidney slowly walked in and stood next to Mr.

Cardini. Their hands were behind their backs. They looked like they were in a police lineup on a TV show.

This was bad.

Really bad.

"As you know," Mr. Cardini said, "Harry and Sidney have been quarreling. After we had a good talk, I found out the boys have been calling each other names. They know it was wrong. They decided on something they could do together, and now they want to show you the results."

I leaned forward to see what it was.

Sidney and Harry each held up a drawing.

Both had drawn pictures of a yellow canary!

Mr. Cardini continued, "I also found

out that the indoor recesses have been taking their toll on Harry, and it got me thinking. If it's okay with Miss Mackle, she can take your class for a five-minute run in the gym when it's available."

"I love the idea!" our teacher said.

Everyone cheered!

Harry was beaming!

"Now, I think Harry has something to say," the principal added.

"I've never seen a real live canary before. I was kind of curious about them. So Sid shared his pet bird book with me. I found out some cool things about them. Miners in England used canaries to find out if there was enough oxygen in the deep mines. Lots of canaries lost their lives so miners could be safe.

And canaries were also used during wartime to detect gases on the battlefields. That changed my opinion about them. Canaries were heroes."

I leaned back in my chair.

I couldn't believe it!

"But there was pandemonium in the office," I blurted out. "Mrs. Carpenter told me that."

Mr. Cardini began to chuckle. "I'd call it a real hullabaloo, yes! Sid's grandpa dropped Cutie Pie off at my office just before lunch. Mrs. Carpenter is bringing him in now."

Everyone gasped as the school secretary walked in carrying a cloth-covered cage. Her hair was combed nicely again, and the black-and-white specks were gone.

"Meet Cutie Pie!" Sid said as he took the cloth off. Cutie Pie was completely yellow except for his black, beady eyes. His talons clung to the perch. He moved his head to the left and then to the right, like he was looking at the class. Everyone could see the mirror and the birdbath in his cage.

Sidney pointed to a white oval hanging in the cage. "That's his cuttlebone. He sharpens his beak with it."

Everyone clapped and cheered.

"Oh Cutie Pie! You are just what Room 3B needs!" Miss Mackle said, beaming.

"Well," Mr. Cardini added, holding up a finger, "a word of warning! Sid wanted to show me how Cutie Pie sits on his finger. Just as the bird was doing that, Mrs. Carpenter came into my office. Cutie Pie didn't like that interruption, I guess, because he started flying all around the room. The four of us were causing quite a commotion trying to catch him. Cutie Pie landed on Mrs. Carpenter's head just long enough to drop something in her hair."

We all knew what *that* was!

When we started to giggle, the principal did too.

"No problem, I'm shampooing well

tonight!" Mrs. Carpenter exclaimed. "It's all in the line of duty."

The principal continued with a chuckle. "So there we were, watching the bird fly around in circles, when he finally landed on something. My orange slices! Harry tiptoed up to Cutie Pie and very carefully cupped his hands over the bird. When he put him back inside the cage, we all cheered."

Song Lee clapped her hands. She was so happy Harry had rescued the bird! The principal could see Harry had a good heart.

"We're all pleased Cutie Pie is safely in his cage. So now you know *not* to open it up. Right, kids?" the principal said with a firm voice.

"Right!" we all repeated.

I was so relieved! Harry wasn't in trouble anymore. He and Sid had actually made peace for once. Now we could get down to business and really study birds. Harry could discover why a vulture can eat decayed dead bodies and not get sick, and I could listen to the sounds different birds make. Best of all, our class would get to take laps in the gym!

Harry did go cuckoo.

I kind of went cuckoo too, worrying about him.

That happens sometimes in the middle of a very cold winter when you're cooped up inside.

Epilogue: What Harry Found Out about Vultures

When it was finally Harry's turn to be the VIP, he shared his report on vultures from the director's chair. He shocked everyone with his presentation.

"You probably wonder why I brought a garbage can to school today. Well, my report is in it. It's called 'Eaters of the Dead.'"

Mary made a face. She didn't like the title, or the poster Harry had made of a vulture on the front of the can. The bird had blood and animal guts in his mouth.

We all watched Harry untape eight strips of paper from the top of the lid. There was a fact written on each one.

EATERS OF THE DEAD
by Harry Spooger

1. Vultures are birds that live all over the world. They are related to eagles and hawks.
2. Most vultures do not kill animals. They eat the meat from animals that are already dead. That's what carrion is—dead meat.
3. Vultures have hooked beaks and strong claws for tearing meat and tough skin.

4. Turkey vultures are really cool. They scare away their enemies by vomiting.

5. Vultures are bald. Since they have no feathers on their heads, blood and flesh don't stick to them, and they can keep clean.

6. Vultures have a digestive system that can process rotten meat.

7. Some vultures pee on their legs to clean off the rotten food. Urine has ammonia in it, and that prevents them from getting an infection. The pee also cools them off.

8. Vultures are the best garbage collectors. They leave only clean bones. When a vulture finishes his job, there is no more decayed meat with germs lying around. That means

our planet Earth is cleaner. And it means that you and I will get fewer diseases.

When Harry finished, he retaped the eight strips of paper back on the garbage lid. "I think vultures are the king of birds!" he said, slapping the can several times.

Everyone clapped for Harry's great presentation.

Even Mary.

"That was just wonderful, Harry!" Miss Mackle exclaimed. "And now, I think we all could use a good run in the gym."

"*Yahoo!*" Harry and I shouted.